HARBINGERS 1

The Call

Bill Myers

Frank Peretti, Angela Hunt, and Alton Gansky

Published by Amaris Media International

Cover Design: Angela Hunt

Photo © Vitaly Krivosheev—Fotolia.com

ISBN: 0692378332
ISBN-13: 978-0692378335

For more information, visit us on Facebook:
https://www.facebook.com/pages/Harbingers/705107309586877

For Angie Hunt: The Wendy to our Peter Pan.

HARBINGERS

A novella series by

Bill Myers, Frank Peretti, Angela Hunt, and Alton Gansky

In this fast-paced world with all its demands, the four of us wanted to try something new. Instead of the longer novel format, we wanted to write something equally as engaging but that could be read in one or two sittings—on the plane, waiting to pick up the kids from soccer, or as an evening's read.

We also wanted to play. As friends and seasoned novelists, we thought it would be fun to create a game we could participate in together. The rules were simple:

Rule #1

Each of us would write as if we were one of the characters in the series:

Bill Myers would write as Brenda, the street-hustling tattoo artist who sees images of the future.

Frank Peretti would write as the professor, the atheist ex-priest ruled by logic.

Angela Hunt would write as Andi, the professor's brilliant-but-geeky assistant who sees inexplicable patterns.

Alton Gansky would write as Tank, the naïve, big-hearted jock with a surprising connection to a healing power.

Rule #2

Instead of the four of us writing one novella together (we're friends but not crazy), we would write it like a TV series. There would be an overarching story line into which we'd plug our individual novellas, with each story written from our character's point of view.

Bill's first novella, *The Call*, sets the stage. It will be followed by Frank's, *The Haunted*, Angela's *The Sentinels*, and Alton's *The Girl*. And if we keep having fun, we'll begin a second round and so on until other demands pull us away or, as in TV, we get cancelled.

There you have it. We hope you'll find these as entertaining in the reading as we did in the writing.

Bill, Frank, Angie, and Al

Chapter 1

There's four of us. Well, five if you count the kid. We don't know each other, we don't like each other, and we sure didn't ask for any of this. But here we are. "The probability of fate," Andi calls it.

I call it a pain in the butt.

Anyway, we each got our own version of what's been happening, so here's mine . . .

It was Friday night. I was tired and business was slow. Time to shut down. I was already cleaning tips and grips when three white boys, football jocks from the community college, roll in. They'd played some big game earlier and it must have been a sweet victory by the way they waved around their Buds and staggered in, giggling. Well, two staggered in giggling—the one they carried between them was barely coherent.

"Hey there, Brenda." The buzz cut on the right had been a recent customer.

I glanced up from where I'm cleaning my stuff. "Sorry, boys all closed up."

He acted like he didn't hear. "We got ourselves an honest to goodness virgin."

The one in the middle, six-three, 275, raised his head and open his watery eyes just long enough to greet me with a Texas drawl, "Ma'am," before nodding back off. But it wasn't the good ol' boy charm that got me. It was the face. The same one I'd been sketching for over a week.

Buzz Cut laughed. "Twenty years old and not a mark on him."

"Pure as driven snow," his buddy agreed.

I looked at the clock. Like I said, business was slow and I was getting tired of ducking the landlord. "You got money?"

All grins, Buzz Cut dug into his pocket and pulled out a wad of cash.

I swore under my breath and motioned them to the beat-up barber chair in the middle of the room. "Set him there."

They plopped him down.

I popped a sterilized pack and began prepping a tip. "What do you have in mind?"

"You know," Buzz Cut said. "Do your hocus-pocus thing."

"My what?"

"Where you tat out his future. Like you did me." He pulled up his sleeve to show a broken heart spurting blood from a bullet shooting through it. "I'm gonna be a heartbreaker, man." He grinned at his buddy. "A real lady killer. Ain't that right, Brenda?"

"If you say so."

"Chicks go for a man in uniform. Wherever they send me I'm gonna leave a long line of broken hearts."

I rolled up Cowboy's sleeve and started prepping the arm.

"So do the same for him," Buzz Cut said. "Tat out his future."

"You really do that?" his pal said.

I reached for a blade and began shaving the arm. "I just ink what I see."

"Well, shoot, do my future, too."

"You ain't got one."

"Huh?"

They both laugh, thinking it's sarcasm. I wish it was.

I sterilize and goop the arm, all the time staring at it.

"So how much?" Buzz Cut says.

"Free form?" It was a lie. Like I said, I'd been sketching stencils for a week. But they didn't have to know.

"Sure."

"Two fifty," I said. "Half now, half on completion."

"So that's . . ."

Thinking wasn't his specialty, so I gave him a hand. "One hundred fifty now, one hundred fifty when the job's done."

"Sweet."

He peeled off the bills, counting as he set them in my palm. "Fifty, one hundred, one hundred fifty."

He figured he was done, but like I said it was a slow week and he was a slow thinker. I gave him a look and glanced at my hand, making it clear he was short.

"Oh, right." He peeled off another fifty.

"I gotta piss," his buddy said.

Buzz Cut nods. He motions to the empty bottle in his hand. "And it's time for a recharge."

His buddy leans over Cowboy and says, "Don't go nowhere pal, we'll be right back."

Buzz Cut adds, "Get some sleep. It'll be over 'fore you know it."

Cowboy doesn't answer, so he shakes him. "Hey . . . hey."

He opens his eyes.

"Get some sleep."

He nods and drops back off.

The boys turned and headed for the door. I stared at the arm, pretending to wait for an image to form. But as soon as they're gone, I crossed to the desk and pulled out the stencil I'd been working on— four grownups and a ten-year old kid walking toward us. I didn't recognize the kid or two of the adults. But, like I said, I recognized Cowboy. And I recognized the woman beside him. Black. A few years older. Dreadlocks. A dead ringer for me.

The job took less than an hour. Another hour passed and still no one showed. It was late and I'd had it. I tossed down the magazine. I butted out my cigarette and crossed over to him. He was snoring like a chain saw.

I shook him. "Hey."

He kept snoring. I shook harder. "Hey!"

He opened one eye, gave a polite "Howdy," and went back to sleep.

I shook him again. "Your friends? Where're your friends?"

Nothing.

Enough was enough. I lifted his arm and slipped under it. Getting him to his feet wasn't as easy.

"Come on, come on," I said. "A little help wouldn't hurt."

Somehow I got him to the door. I hit the lights with my elbow, staggered outside and leaned him against the wall to lock up. I barely got out my keys before he started sliding.

"No, no, no—"

He hit the sidewalk with a thud. I finished locking up and knelt down to him. "Hey. Hey, Cowboy."

Nothing.

"Okay, fine." Prattville was safe enough. A small town in the middle of the desert. And the night was warm. He could just sit there 'til his buddies remembered where they left him.

I turned and headed toward my beater Toyota. Once I got there, I reached through the window to open the door. I glanced back at him. Big mistake. He sat there all alone and helpless looking.

I swore and started back.

Two minutes later I'm loading him into the passenger seat. He does his best to help, which was next to nothing. Once all the arms and legs are inside, I got behind the wheel. "Okay, Cowboy," I said, "where to?"

He mumbled something.

I shook my head and sighed.

Suddenly the car shook as something roared overhead. I stuck my head out the window just in time to see a private jet shoot by. It was 300 feet above us, with smoke and flames coming from its engine.

I looked around, then dropped the car into gear and hit the gas.

Chapter 2

The jet took its sweet time to come down. We'd been on the road fifteen minutes and still hadn't found it. But we would. I saw the direction it was going and doubted it would be making any turns. I'd have called someone, but as usual my crap phone battery was dead.

"Where . . . are we?"

I turned to see Cowboy coming to. "Well, look who joined us. Hope you got cash. Door to door delivery is extra."

He frowned. "Sorry?"

"I'm driving you home."

He managed to turn his head and look out the window. "But . . . I don't live out here."

"We're taking the scenic route."

He sat up. "That's real kind of you, but—" He spotted the cellophane over the tat and pulled at it. "*Ow!*"

"Yeah, that's going to be a little tender," I said.

He looked at it. "Wow. Did you all do that? That's real nice. Who are them people?"

"No idea." I glanced at it. "That big guy's you, obviously. But those others . . ." I shrugged.

"What about—Ow!" He'd touched it again. "Her?"

"What about her?"

"She kinda looks like you?"

"What do you mean, 'kinda?' That's a great likeness."

"Watch out!"

I turned back to the road just in time to see some old dude and a girl. I yanked the wheel to the right, swerving, barely missing them. Well, mostly missing them. I must of clipped the old guy, cause the next thing I know, he's out of sight.

I slammed on the brakes. The car barely stopped before I leapt out of it. He was on the ground twenty feet behind.

"Are you all right?" I shouted, racing to him, "You okay?"

"Professor?" The girl, a twenty-something redhead, was already at his side. I could only see her back. "Professor!"

He was sitting up when I got there. Even in the moonlight, I recognized the face. It set me back, but not much. When you sketch like me, you're never too surprised when the stuff shows up.

He was the third person in Cowboy's tattoo. His neatly trimmed beard and silver hair made him look like a senator, all polite and genteel . . . until he opened his mouth.

"Moron!" he shouted. "There's nothing but desert out here and you couldn't see us?"

"Sorry," I said.

"What type of idiot are you?"

"I didn't see—"

"Stupid women drivers."

"What?"

"You heard me."

Normally, I'd be sympathetic, 'specially with not paying my insurance the last couple years. But he was a real piece of work. "Maybe if you didn't walk down the middle of the highway, you'd be easier to miss."

"A highway, is that what you call it?" He tried moving his leg and winced.

"Professor—"

"You people should try using some asphalt, or put a white line somewhere so we'd have a clue."

"Professor, you're hurt."

"I'm fine." He winced again.

The girl bent closer. Little Orphan Annie curls blocked her face.

"Were you with the plane?" I asked.

He didn't bother to answer. "How far are we from town?"

"Were you with the pla—?"

"Are you okay?" Cowboy interrupted as he joined us. "It looks like you're hurt."

The old man shot him a glare then turned back to the girl. "Are mental midgets the only indigenous life form here?"

Cowboy smiled that dumb smile of his and kneeled down to join us.

The girl kept checking his leg. "We were flying to UCLA. That's where the professor will be delivering his next set of lectures. They're very informative and the reviews have been extremely positive." She looked up at me, shaking back those curls as she kept chattering. But I barely heard. I was looking directly into face number four.

"So our engine experienced some mechanical difficulties, at about—" she looked at her watch— "actually, exactly one hour and eight minutes ago. And the pilots, nice men both of them—an older gentlemen with a moustache and a younger one who forgot to button his fourth shirt button from the top— decided to set the plane down back there—" she motioned over her shoulder— "approximately one point two miles—"

"Incompetent boneheads." The old man tested his leg again and winced.

"They okay?" I asked. "The pilots?"

"Until I sue them for attempted manslaughter."

"Professor, they saved our lives."

"Which they'll live to regret."

"No one injured?"

"Everyone's fine," the girl said. "They're flying in a mechanic first thing in the morning and they called a taxi for us."

"But you didn't wait."

The professor answered. "I've developed serious trust issues with them in the matter of transpor— Ahh!" He turned to Cowboy, who'd put a hand on his leg. "What are you doing?"

"Sorry," the big guy said.

The professor turned to me. "So do you have hospitals out here? Or do you just leave people on the side of the road until they expire?" He spun back to Cowboy who was touching him again. "What are you . . . where's that heat coming from?"

"Sorry."

He looked to the girl. "Andi, get on the phone and call 911. Tell them I expect a vehicle to be sent immediately and—" He stopped and shouted at Cowboy again. "What's that heat? What are you doing?"

Cowboy gave no answer and the old man pulled his leg away.

"That's strange," he said.

"Professor?"

He moved it. "What on earth?" He reached down, touched the leg, then moved it some more. "How very odd."

"What's wrong?"

He didn't answer but kept testing his leg. Finally, he rolled over onto his hands and knees.

"Professor, be careful, you're hurt."

"Nonsense." With some effort he managed to stand.

The girl took his arm. "Please, Professor, we don't know what's—"

"I'm fine." He shrugged her off. "Let go. I said I'm fine. I must have pulled something." He began walking. "See, I'm fine now."

I glanced at Cowboy, who avoided my gaze.

"So, how far to the nearest town?" the old man demanded.

"Nine, ten miles," I said.

"Good. Then you will take us to your finest hotel—provided, of course, you are able to stay on the road without hitting anyone or anything else."

I turned for the car. "Let's go, Cowboy."

"Don't worry," the old man said. "We'll pay."

"I'm not a taxi service."

"Twenty-five dollars."

I turned. "You think you can just buy me like some—"

"Fifty."

"Seventy-five."

"Don't be absurd."

I continued toward the car.

"Surely you don't intend to leave us out here."

"Enjoy the walk."

"All right, all right," he said. "Seventy-five."

"Per person."

"That's robbery!"

"Take it or leave it."

He stood, anything but happy.

I shrugged, knowing I had him. "That's how us mental midgets do business."

Chapter 3

Cowboy, because of his size, sat up front with me. The professor, because of his mouth, sat in the back with Andi.

But that didn't stop Cowboy's downhome charm. "So, how come you're a professor and all, but you ain't teaching at a college?"

Andi, who had the enthusiasm of a fourteen-year-old and energy to back it up, answered. "He's on a national lecture tour. Lots of universities. Come next Spring we've even been invited to the White House."

Cowboy grinned. "You don't say."

"And before that we're going to the Middle East

and Europe. Maybe even the Vatican."

"That sounds real nice. And what, exactly, do you all lecture on?"

The professor didn't answer, which didn't stop Cowboy. "S'cuse me, Professor, what did you say your lectures are about?"

More silence.

"Professor?"

Finally the old man said, "What's your name, son?"

"Bjorn Christiansen. They call me Tank for short."

"Well, Tank for short, during this lovely tour of your desolate countryside, do you suppose for one minute we could enjoy some silence?"

I shot the man a look in the mirror.

Miss Congeniality answered. "The professor lectures on the toxicity of believing in God in a post-modern culture."

Cowboy stayed quiet, which I got to admit was a bit of a relief. But it didn't last long.

"I'm sorry. I don't mean to be rude or nothin', but why do you want to go around telling people there ain't a God?"

"I don't tell them there isn't a God. I tell them they're intellectually stunted if they believe in one."

Cowboy frowned. "But I believe in God."

"Yes, I'm sure you do."

I glanced back in the mirror. "So you're an atheist," I said.

"I'm a realist."

"You tour the world to mess up people's faith?"

"I tour the world as penance for the lives I've ruined."

"He was a priest," Andi explained. "A Jesuit."

"That was a long, long time ago," he said.

"But—" Cowboy turned back to him. "I'm confused."

"I'm sure you are."

"If you're a priest how come you don't believe—"

"Stop the car!" Andi shouted. "Quick, stop the car!"

If it was the professor who yelled, I wouldn't of bothered. But the girl I almost liked, in spite of her perkiness.

"What's up?" I said as we slowed.

"There!" She pointed off to the right. "Over there."

A hundred yards away, you could see pillars of rock shining in the moonlight. Like giant stalagmites. Some rose a hundred feet high. Around them were a bunch of buildings, a fancy school I had some history with.

"Those are the Trona Pinnacles," Cowboy said. "Kinda famous around here."

"There's nine of them, right?" Andi asked.

"That's what you see from the road," I said "but there's plenty more"

"And this is September sixth." She turned to the old man. "Nine, six, Professor."

"Please, I am in no mood for your—"

"And what time did our plane leave?"

"Andi . . ."

"We were supposed to leave at eight o'clock."

He sighed. "But because of mechanical difficulties we were delayed an hour."

"Actually one hour and six minutes."

"Andrea-

"Putting our departure time at—"

"Ms. Goldstein—"

"9:06."

He looked at me in the mirror. "She has a thing for numbers."

"Not just numbers," she said. "Patterns. Everything's a pattern. The Fibonacci Numerical Series and the Golden Ratio, DNA, Scale Rotational Crystal Growth. Please stop the car."

The professor sighed. "Better do as she says."

I pulled to a stop in the school's driveway, under its sign.

"What are those buildings?" Andi asked.

"Some hot-shot, prep-school for geniuses."

She squinted at the sign. "The Institute for Advanced Psychic Studies."

"Like I said, it's a—"

"That's six words!" she cried.

"Andi—"

"And the date! Look at the date!"

Locals who never got over the Institute buying up the place used the sign for target practice. But you could still read the date it was built. At least part of it.

"-996!" Andi practically shouted.

"Excuse me?" I heard another voice, from outside. I glanced at my side mirror and saw some skinny teen walking toward us.

"Wonderful," the professor sighed. "More local color."

The kid came up to my open window. "Where have you been?" He had an accent like he should be working in a Seven-Eleven.

"I know you?" I said.

"I am Sridhar. Sridhar Rajput."

He stood a moment, then reached out to shake my

hand. I didn't feel inclined to take it. "What can I do for you Sridhar Rajput?"

"It has been three hours." His voice cracked. Sounded like nerves. "I have been waiting nearly three hours for you to come and address my concerns."

"Waiting?"

"My dreams, they indicated you would be here at 11:00 PM and now it is nearly 2:00."

Chapter 4

As we headed down the Institute's drive, the kid dumped a truckload of info on us. Most of it I already knew and I'll tell you about in a minute. Of course, the professor, in his usual charming manner, made it clear he didn't buy any of it.

"So why you coming with us?" I said. "If you think the place is a crock, you should have stayed in the car."

"I have no inclination to sit alone in some godforsaken desert waiting to be mugged or run over again."

Of course it was a lie. He was as curious as the rest

of us.

The Institute had always been a mystery. Our private Area 51. It started back when some geologists tried digging a well into the Earth's mantle. They got nine miles down when the drill started to wobble, then flew out of control. They said they'd hit a giant cavern and couldn't go on. Maybe they did, maybe they didn't. Whatever the reason, there was plenty of talk about smelling sulfur and hearing voices. Some claimed they heard animals howling. Others said people.

The point is, they shut down the place until another organization came along and bought it. They built the fancy boarding school. Once in a while we see a teacher or student from it, but for the most part they stick to themselves. They don't bother us and we don't bother them. No one gives them a thought, except for the rumors--everything from a vacation spot for extraterrestrials to an assembly plant of spare body parts for super heroes.

Truth is, like the sign says, it's a place where they study psychic stuff. They fly kids in from all over the world who are supposed to be gifted. I don't care how you cut it, for me that makes the place interesting. That's why when some kid appears in the middle of the night begging us to follow him and check something out . . . well, here I am.

We were twenty yards from the main gate and guardhouse when I said, "You guys had to take lots of tests to get in?"

"Yes, we have had many examinations. Physical, psychological, intellectual. They even studied our DNA."

I nodded. "To make sure you were worth the

investment."

"That is correct. But you must not feel bad. You came extremely close."

"Say what?"

"You think I would not know? I did my homework, Brenda Barnick."

I gave him a look. The Institute was the reason I dropped out of school and moved here in the first place. With the pictures and stuff I see, I figured I might get in. No such luck. But that was a long time ago."

"And you." The kid turned to Cowboy.

"Me?"

"Did you ever wonder why a small community college would offer a football scholarship to a student three states away?"

Cowboy shrugged. "Some folks think I'm kinda good."

"They wanted him nearby?" I asked. "They paid the college to bring him here?"

"So they could monitor him, that is correct."

"We got a pretty good season so far," Cowboy said.

Andi spoke up. "When you use the term, 'they,' who, exactly, do you mean?"

"Dr. Trenton, our director, calls them *the Gate*. Though I believe even he is not entirely sure who they are. We are merely their training camp. One of several. They are very secretive and—" he lowered his voice—"that is one of my many concerns."

"Right," she said. "You mentioned concerns."

"Which is why you have come."

We traded looks with each other.

"Please," he said. "I am not complaining. It is a

great privilege to attend here. My parents could not be more proud. And the placement they offer after graduation, you cannot imagine. Nevertheless . . . well, you shall see. My dreams said you would come to help me decide, and I trust my dreams."

"Of course," the professor said dryly, "that explains everything."

"When did you first come here?" Cowboy asked.

"Our gifts surface during adolescence. Precognitive skills, psychokinesis, astral projection, telepathy—"

"And in your case, dreaming," Andi said.

"Yes. Originally it was lucid dreaming. But with my concentrated training it has grown much greater. And after the induction service tomorrow, it will become so great I shall be able to serve the nations."

"Nations?" Andi said.

"One of last year's students graduated in my same area of expertise. She now lives in Brussels and assists the European Banking Federation."

"The Illuminati all filled up?" the professor asked.

Andi ignored him. "And you? Where will you go after graduation?"

He looked down. "That is why you are here. The ceremony will be tomorrow and—"

"Tomorrow?"

"—and I am not entirely sure of its safety. The Institute can be quite strict and demanding."

"Which is why they allow you to wander off campus anytime you wish," the professor said.

"Not exactly." The kid lowered his head and pushed back the hair on the back of his neck. There, at the base of his skull, was a piece of metal the size of a dime. It glowed and pulsed a faint blue.

"Is that some sort of tracking device?" the professor said.

The kid nodded.

"They know you're here?" Andi asked.

He smiled. "Yes and no. Come." He motioned us to the guard shack. Once we got there, Sridhar opened the door and we stepped inside. The place looked like something out of a sci-fi film—rows of flashing lights, TV monitors, and other high-tech junk. Some Arnold Schwarzenegger-wannabe was asleep in front of the control board. The TV screen directly in front of him was playing a cheap porn flick. But he was sound asleep—head tilted back on the chair, headphones over his ears, snoring away.

"Security at its finest," the professor said.

"Actually, I provided a little help." The kid reached into his pocket and pulled out a bottle of some over-the-counter sleeping aid.

"You slipped him a sleeping pill?" I said.

"Actually, three. At his request."

"Guys," Cowboy said, "I really don't think we should be here."

I glanced over and saw him staring at the floor. "Why not?"

Without looking, he gestured to the porn flick.

"Does that embarrass you?" Andi asked.

"No, ma'am. But if it's just the same with you—" he started toward the door—"I'll just step outside 'til you're all done here." Before we could answer, he headed back out into the night.

Andi turned to the kid. "I'm still confused. Why would the guard ask you to put him to sleep?"

Sridhar pointed to a set of eight monitors to the right. Each had six photos of kids with a few statistics printed under them. I stepped closer to look. The photo of Sridhar was flashing red.

"That indicates I have stepped off the grounds," he said.

"And?"

"Not only can I manipulate my own dreams, but I've learned to manipulate others. Mr. Hanson—the guard—has agreed to let me leave the grounds if I provide him with enough . . . incentive."

"Sleeping pills and a porn flick?" I said.

"I have directed his dreams to experience everything he hears in the movie."

"As if he's living it?"

"Precisely. In his dream, he is immersed in the movie as if he is there, as if it is really happening to him."

"That's sick," Andi said.

I shrugged. "Sounds like a win/win to me. You get what you want and so does the Incredible Hulk here."

"Except—" the kid hesitated. "He is never satisfied. Each time he insists upon more explicit material. It is becoming increasingly difficult to meet such demands."

"Everyone has his weakness," the professor said, moving to study the switches on the board.

The kid sighed. "Which we are carefully taught to exploit." He hit a button on the panel. The iron gate in front began to open. "Come, we haven't much time."

"Before?"

"Dr. Trenton discovers you are here."

"How will he know?" I nodded to the sleeping guard.

"The Travelers will awaken him."

"Travelers?"

He didn't answer, just motioned for us to follow. We stepped outside and joined Cowboy who was humming, hands in his pockets, and gazing up at the stars. We headed towards the opening gate.

"That's it for your security?" the professor said.

"Pardon me?"

"A fence, some security cameras, and a sleeping pervert? Out here in the middle of the desert I would have expected more."

"As I said, we are merely a training facility. However, we do have one further line of defense."

The gate finished opening and we stepped through.

Chapter 5

The grounds were like I remembered. A couple of three-story buildings to our left, two more to our right, and a smaller round one straight ahead. The stone pillars rose between them. Some were as wide as thirty feet. Others ten. Some twenty feet tall. Others over a hundred.

It all felt very familiar and very strange. Stranger still was the kid stopping to put on a pair of John Lennon granny glasses.

He saw us looking at him and explained. "They reveal the location of the security field that is repositioned every week."

"Security field?" Cowboy asked.

"It is an energy field that scans the brain waves of any intruder. It reads their greatest fears, then runs them through a central computer that amplifies them. They are then broadcast back into the brain many times stronger."

"Of course," the professor said. "One of those."

"What I wish to show you is in the auditorium just ahead. But you must stay behind me and follow my route. You must not leave the path I follow." He turned to the right, and walked almost parallel to the fence.

Me and Andi traded looks, then followed. So did Cowboy.

Not our resident cynic.

Andi was the first to notice. "Professor?"

"You're going to this building less than fifty feet in front of us, correct?"

"That is correct."

"So why the circular route?"

"As I said, you must follow the prescribed path or you will—"

The professor snorted and started walking straight ahead.

"Doctor, no!" Sridhar called. "You must not do that!"

"Watch me."

"Doctor—"

Nothing happened, at first. Two, three, four steps. Nothing. Then the old man slowed and looked down.

"Professor?"

He turned to us. "What's going on?"

"Doctor—"

"My mind . . . it's—"

"Doctor, you must step out of there. Step out of the field and follow—"

"It's—" his face filled with concern. "I can't . . . I'm . . . my thoughts, I can't—" He grabbed his head. "What's happening?"

Sridhar stepped around us and doubled back, careful to stay on the path.

"I don't . . . I—"

"Professor!"

He looked up, his eyes wide. "Help me . . . I can't—" He bent down, still holding his head. "I'm . . . I can't remember."

"It is an illusion." The kid stepped as close to him as he dared. "It's what you fear most."

"My memories, they're . . . Sartre. Jean-Paul Sartre. He stated that . . . in 1890 he stated . . . No, that wasn't Sartre. He wasn't born until . . . ahh, I can't . . . when did Sartre live?"

Andi called to Sridhar. "Do something. Help him."

The kid shook his head. "No one can go in there. He must—"

"Kierkegaard, Soren Kierke—what did he, who?" He looked up at Sridhar. "Help me."

"You cannot fight it, Doctor. You cannot fight fear. You can only replace it."

"I don't understand!"

Andi started toward him. I grabbed her arm and shook my head.

Sridhar spotted us. "Stay there. You must stay on the path."

"Pi." The professor looked around in panic. "Three point one four one—" He stopped. "Three point one—three—I can't, I can't remember pi!"

"Doctor, listen to me." The kid tried to sound

calm, but wasn't doing so good. "We can not fight our fears, we can only replace them."

"I don't—"

"Think of something good. You must think of something pleasant to replace your fears, something you really enjoy."

"I enjoy my intelligence."

Sridhar shook his head. "No. A place. An activity."

"I don't—Books, I like to learn. I like—"

"No. A person. Is there a person you are fond of? Just one person."

"Better try another approach," Andi said.

"I . . . She was a long time ago."

"Who? When?"

"Mindy . . . Mindy Buchanan. Junior High."

"Think of Mindy Buchanan. What did she look like?"

He closed his eyes, frowning.

"Think of her clothes. Her hair."

He kept thinking.

"Good . . . that's good."

The professor opened his eyes and looked at Sridhar in surprise.

"That's right," the kid said. "Keep thinking about Mindy. Think about Mindy and start moving toward me."

The old man nodded and took a step. Then another.

"Her voice," the kid said. "Remember what her voice sounded like."

The professor slowed, then stopped. He was three or four feet from Sridhar, but couldn't move.

"What's wrong?"

"She called me . . . stupid." The man scowled.

"She said I wasn't smart enough."

"No, no. Think of the good."

"She said I'd never amount to—" He cringed.

"No, Doctor."

He grabbed his head. "I . . . can't remember."

"Professor!"

"What did . . . I . . . can't."

There was no way he could go on. He was so close, but there was no way he—

Suddenly, without warning, the kid leaped off the path. He stepped into the field and grabbed the professor by the arm.

"What are you doing?" the professor shouted. "What are you—"

The kid tried dragging him out. When that didn't work, he ran behind the professor and pushed, slamming the man hard into his back. They both fell out of the field and onto the ground, the kid on top of him.

"What are you doing?" the professor yelled.

"I was—"

"Get off me, you ignoramus! Clumsy oaf. Get off! Get off!"

The kid scrambled away. The professor got to his feet, then brushed off his slacks and adjusted his sports coat, grumbling all the way.

He'd obviously made a full recovery.

Chapter 6

The auditorium had two, maybe three hundred seats. At one end there was a stage with a lectern. Behind the lectern sat six high back chairs with armrests. Behind them were a couple of risers. And in front of the stage was another platform, more like a cube. Five by five by five. Bronze. In the center was a sealed pipe that stuck out another six or so inches.

I turned to Sridhar. "Is that—"

"Yes, that is the well."

"And those chairs?" Andi asked. "Up on the stage?"

"That is where we will sit for tomorrow's

graduation. Mine is the sixth and final one to the right."

"Six?" Andi said. "Did you hear that, Professor? There are six graduates."

The professor ignored her. He'd spotted a large control board at the back of the auditorium and was heading up the steps to check it out.

Earlier, when we followed Sridhar and the spiraling path into the building, Cowboy wouldn't come in. He just stood at the side door in the hallway that surrounded the auditorium.

"What's wrong?" I said.

"The place gives me the willies."

"Like the guard shack?"

"No. Yes. Different. Yeah, but kinda the same."

I shook my head, then turned to the kid. "What's the deal with the well?"

"It is sealed for now," he said. "But during tomorrow's induction, it shall be opened."

"And why is that?" Andi said.

"It is best that I show you." He turned to the center of the auditorium and called, "Computer. Please play last year's ceremony."

The air above the middle of the room sparkled, then filled with light. Suddenly we were looking at a 3-D hologram of the auditorium filled with people. This time, up on the stage, there were eight kids."

"That is last year's class," Sridhar said.

The students looked comfortable enough, all prim and proper in their white gowns. You barely noticed their wrists strapped to the armrests or their ankles strapped to the legs of the chairs. On the risers behind them stood a dozen younger kids. Up at the lectern, some pompous, slick dude in a three-piece suit was giving a speech:

" . . . leaving selfish ambition behind to enter a new fraternity, an order that will guide us from the old paradigms of self-centeredness and destruction into a new era of peace, wisdom and freedom."

The audience clapped.

"Computer," Sridhar called, "go to the induction."

The image flickered. Now the students on the risers were singing. One of those Medieval chant things, only higher and creepier. As they sang, two older dudes, dressed in red robes, came up to the cubicle. They carried a long, silver pole that they slipped into the ring on the pipe's lid. Then, as one stood at each end of the pole, they lifted the lid.

"Come," the slick speaker called. "Travelers of the future, come fill these newest vessels with your ceaseless knowledge."

The singing grew louder and creepier. Wisps of green smoke started rising from the pipe. It grew thicker until it became a green cloud that glowed and pulsed with the music. It rose until it was ten feet above the cube.

"Guys," Cowboy yelled over the music. "I don't like this."

I glanced over my shoulder. He had inched his way into the auditorium a few feet.

The cloud drifted over to the stage. As it did, it divided in half. Then those halves split again, so there were four. They split again, so there were eight. Eight little clouds pulsing in perfect unison to the music.

"Guys?"

The clouds drifted until each one floated over a graduate. The students watched, not quite as relaxed as before.

"The time has arrived," Slick shouted over the singing. "All of your hard work and diligence shall be rewarded. Now is the time to reap your reward. Now is the time for induction."

The singing amped up until it almost sounded like screaming. The students kept staring up at their clouds.

"And so, let it begin!"

The clouds began to churn. The music got louder. Finally, one of the kids opened her mouth. Wide. And she kept it open.

"Come," Slick called. "Now is the time."

Another opened his mouth. And then another. And another. They looked like baby chicks waiting to be fed. The clouds kept pulsing and churning until the last kid opened his. Then Slick shouted:

"Receive your destiny!"

In a flash, the clouds shot into their mouths. At first the kids resisted. They rocked back and forth, pulling against the straps holding their hands and ankles. If they screamed, you couldn't hear it over the music.

It only lasted only a few seconds. Pretty soon they stopped fighting and relaxed. One by one, they closed their mouths and lowered their heads. They looked calmly out over the audience.

And the crowd broke into cheers and applause.

"Hologram, off." Sridhar said.

The image disappeared and we stood in the silence, trying to digest it all.

Finally Cowboy spoke. "It's the devil."

I turned to him.

"Those are demons straight from the pit of hell," he said.

"Demons?" Sridhar sounded surprised. "Dr. Trenton says they are time travelers. They have returned in time through a portal in the earth's crust to warn us and save our planet."

I turned back to Cowboy. "So you don't think Sridhar should be a part of this?"

"I don't think we should even be inside this room."

"Andi—" the professor shouted down from the console. "Can you come up here a moment?"

"It's creepy," I said to Cowboy. "I'll give you that. And those kids on stage weren't exactly thrilled."

"Until their training took over," Sridhar said. "After the initial shock they were fine. Better than fine."

"And you've talked to them?" I said. "Afterwards?"

"Yes. Many are my good friends and now they work closely with world leaders. Everything is well and good."

"Except for them being possessed," Cowboy said.

"Guys?" Andi called from the console. "Check it out." She hit a few switches and motioned to the stage.

The same smoke we'd seen in the hologram was rising from the pipe. Only this time the pipe was covered.

"That's not possible," the kid said. "The well won't be unsealed until tomorrow."

"Looks like it has different plans." I moved in closer for a look.

"Miss Brenda—" Cowboy warned.

By the time I got to the cube, I saw something wasn't right. It took a moment to work up my courage, but I finally stretched my hand into the smoke. Only there *was* no smoke. My hand lit up green and I could see smoke on it, but there was no smoke. I wiggled my fingers. I waved. Nothing. It was just a projection.

The professor called down from the console. "Behold your demons."

I pulled back my hand and turned to him. "Another hologram?"

Andi flipped a couple of switches on the console. The smoke rose and pulsed just like before. It divided. First into two clouds, than four, then the last one divided again, making six. They drifted until one floated over each of the chairs.

"It's a light show," I said. "Just special effects."

"But—" the kid moved beside me. "What about the graduates?"

"What about them?" the professor said.

"Surely, you saw their reaction when the travelers first entered them."

"I saw eight susceptible teenagers programmed for months, perhaps years, to believe whatever they saw and heard."

"But . . . our training, our classes—"

"Take a good look, son. It's all smoke and mirrors."

"Not entirely."

I spun around to see Slick himself standing in the center of the stage.

Chapter 7

"Dr. Trenton." Sridhar took a step toward the stage. "I am so sorry. Let me explain. I was—"

Slick held up his hand and the kid stopped. Then the man turned to me. "Ms. Barnick, it's so good to see you again."

It took me back, but I held my ground. "We never met. I don't know you."

"You may not know me, but I certainly know you." He shoved his hands into his pockets, all relaxed. "So tell me, how's life as a tattoo artist?"

I nodded toward the clouds. "How's your life as a con artist?"

He smiled, all superior like. "Yes." He called to the back of the auditorium, "Andrea? Would you be so kind as to shut that down, please? It can be so distracting."

"How do you know my name?" Andi called.

"The controls are to your left. But apparently you've already discovered them."

"Yes, I have, and they're very impressive." She punched a few buttons and the clouds disappeared. "But how did—"

"Thank you. And Dr. James McKinney, tell me, what do you think?"

The professor was unfazed. "Time travelers? Is that the best you could come up with?"

"You don't believe in time travel."

The professor motioned to the stage. "Apparently, neither do you."

"Oh, that." Slick chuckled. "It's an audiovisual aide. Merely something for weaker minds to put their faith in."

"So it's all fake?" Andi asked.

"No, dear. It's an icon. As real as the Kaaba in Mecca, the crosses in churches—"

"Or the face of the Virgin Mary in a Burrito," the professor said.

Slick gave that smile again, this time for the professor. "Whether you care to admit it or not, those beliefs, however misinterpreted by the masses, have a trace of truth."

"I prefer my truth less delusional."

"And what truth would that be, Professor? Existentialism? Postmodernism? What's your flavor-of-the-month today?"

"It's certainly not *Star Trek* reruns or wherever

you're getting your inspiration."

"That's right, you're a good eighteenth century scientist, aren't you? A classical materialist who believes only in what he can see."

"I'm a realist. If it can't be measured, it doesn't exist."

"So you have no belief in the multiple dimensions surrounding us."

"No more than the Easter Bunny or Santa Claus."

"Even though theoretical mathematicians have clearly proven them as fact."

"*Theoretical* and *fact* do not belong in the same sentence."

"Like the theory of evolution?"

"Please," the professor scorned.

"Or Dark Matter."

"That's an entirely different issue."

"No, that's 72 percent of reality. And every physicist worth his salt knows it. It can't be touched, it can't be measured, but they know it's here. The same goes for Dark Energy making up an additional 24 percent. So, congratulations, Professor, you believe in 6 percent of reality."

"Who are you really? What's this place about?"

"It's a doorway to our future. As is every student here." He gestured to Sridhar. "Each one carefully trained to bring us back from the brink of extinction and usher in a new age of peace and prosperity for all."

"Break out the incense and love beads."

"Oh, you are a tough one, aren't you." Slick paused, then added, "I believe in—"

At that same moment, the professor said : "I believe in—"

Both men stopped. The professor frowned.

Slick smiled. Then he said, "What are you?" just as the professor said, "What are you?"

Again they stopped. The professor frowned harder.

Slick smiled bigger. Then he said, "What's this?" just as the professor said, "What's this?"

They kept going. "Another one—"

"Another one—"

"Of—"

"Of—"

"Your—"

"Your—"

"Tricks?"

"Tricks?"

The professor was anything but thrilled.

Slick just grinned. "Now how did I know you were going to say that?"

"Actually, that's a very good question," Andi said. She left the console and started down the steps, moving toward the stage. "How *did* you know?"

"I didn't. But the time traveler I'm hosting did. In fact, if I allowed him, he could recite our entire conversation before it began."

He paused then added, "That's ridic—" just as the professor said, "That's ridic—" and stopped.

"Yes." There was that smile again.

Andi joined me at the cube in front of the stage. "So there's absolutely nothing coming out of this tube?" she said. "It's all special effects?"

"Yes and no. The time travelers will be gathered all about this stage tomorrow. The special effects are merely a way of priming the pump, of helping the audience visualize what is actually occurring. The same goes for the graduates. It provides a point of reference so when the indwelling occurs, they are not startled or alarmed."

He turned to the kid. "And Sridhar, I'm afraid this must remain our little secret. As you can imagine, I am not pleased to find you and your friends skulking about, and uncovering such information, especially before our big day. And it may make your own induction tomorrow less pleasant. Nevertheless, it is imperative you not share this with the other graduates."

"Yes, sir."

"The music, these effects, all are designed to create an environment more conducive to receiving your travelers. Without focusing upon them, your natural defenses will resist—a painful penalty for your disobedience. However, there is no need for your fellow graduates to also suffer. Wouldn't you agree?"

"Yes, sir."

He turned back to us. "With or without the assistance of these special effects, the travelers *will* enter the graduates where they will continue to expand each host's giftedness in order to help and enlighten the world."

"Demons," Cowboy called from the doorway. "They're demons sent by the devil himself."

Slick looked at him sadly. "Yes . . . little wonder you weren't admitted into the program." He turned to the rest of us and clapped his hands. "Well, as much fun as this has been, I'm afraid you'll have to come back some other time. Tomorrow's activities start at eleven and it will be a very busy day." He turned to Sridhar. "As for you, my young friend, it's off to bed with you. Try and put that curious mind of yours to rest. Tomorrow will prove to be one of the most important days of your life."

The kid looked at him a moment, then lowered his gaze.

"What if he doesn't want to go?" Andi asked.

"Excuse me?"

"The boy has had second thoughts," the professor added.

"I'm sorry, that's not possible."

"Possible or not, it seems to be—"

Slick made a sharp motion with his hand. The kid grabbed the back of his neck and cried out. "Ahh . . ."

"Is that correct, Sridhar?" Slick asked.

The boy was in too much pain to answer.

"What are you doing?" Andi demanded.

He calmly repeated, "Sridhar? Is that correct."

"I—" the kid gasped.

"What's going on?" Andi cried. "What are you doing?

"An electronic leash," the professor said.

Slick smiled. "Very good."

The professor continued. "Not only does it serve as a tracking device, but apparently as a method of control as well."

"Only for the less compliant," Slick said. "Time to call it a night, son." He waved his hand and the kid cried out again, this time doubling over in pain.

"Stop it," Andi shouted. "You're hurting him!"

"Let him go!" Cowboy 's voice joined with Andi's. "Stop it!"

Sridhar kept gasping. "Please . . . please—"

"Stop it!"

All right. Enough was enough. They could yell all they wanted, but there's only one way to stop a bully.

I took off up the steps and went across the stage, heading straight for him. He had me by twenty, thirty pounds. I had him by surviving the streets.

I heard Cowboy shouting behind me, but I didn't need his help. I lunged at Slick and shot straight through him like he was thin air. The reason was simple. He *was* thin air. Another projection. I spun around and tried again. Same thing. Only now he was laughing.

"Please, Dr. Trenton," the kid begged. "I shall go. Please!"

Slick's projection turned to him.

The kid stood panting. Sweating.

"Go," was all Slick said.

The kid nodded and staggered toward the opposite exit.

"Sridhar!" Andi shouted.

"Big day tomorrow, son," Slick called after him. "Need to get that beauty sleep."

"Wait!" Cowboy shouted. "Hold on, now." He raced toward the boy, but was too late. The kid never looked back as he stepped through the door and let it slam behind him.

"Sridhar!" Cowboy got to the door. Pushed it. Slammed it. Pushed again. It didn't budge.

Andi spun back to Slick's image. "You can't hold him against his will."

"Actually, he looked more than willing, wouldn't you say? And as for you—" He glanced at his watch. "I have deactivated the security field for the next two minutes. That should give you all ample time to leave the auditorium, cross the yard, and exit through the gate."

"And if we don't?" the Professor said.

"Then I shall have you arrested for trespassing and breaking and entering."

"We were invited," Andi argued.

Slick looked to where Sridhar had exited. "That may be difficult to prove." He glanced back at his watch. "One minute forty-four seconds."

We stood a moment. No one knew what to do.

"Better hurry," Slick said. "As the professor can attest, the effects of the field can be quite unpleasant. One minute thirty-two. I believe you have played out all of your cards for this evening, wouldn't you agree?"

The professor was the first to turn. He hesitated, then started for the exit.

"Professor?"

"I'm not going through that field again," he said. "Trust me, none of you want to."

"An excellent choice, sir."

Without warning, Cowboy bolted for the stage.

"No!" I shouted. "He's just a projection." I waved my hand through Slick as a reminder and Cowboy slowed to a stop.

"Seventy-six seconds," Slick said. "Dear me, it will be close."

I looked after the professor then glanced at the others. Finally I turned to leave.

"Miss Brenda, what are you doing?"

"Nothing," I said. "There's nothing any of us can do. At least tonight."

"Very good," Slick called after me. "Run, run, run away; come back to fight some other day."

What I wouldn't give for him to be real. Just long enough to land one punch. But he wasn't real and there was nothing we could do.

Those were the facts. The same facts that led Andi to eventually turn and follow me. And finally, Cowboy.

We stepped outside and barely made it across the field in time. A groggy guard had opened the gate and we walked through. It closed with a mournful creak, followed by a dull thud.

We headed back to my car. Nobody said a word. Nobody wanted to. We were all alone with just our thoughts and the dark, violet band stretching across the horizon.

Chapter 8

I wanna make it clear, I'm no pushover. Just because some kid I don't know gets into something over his head, doesn't make it my business. It happens all the time. Hookers, gang members, drug runners . . . if they can get out, fine. If not, it's called survival of the fittest.

Despite Cowboy's whining and Miss Do-gooder's pleadings I'd had enough. And for the first time I could remember, me and the professor agreed. Of course we'd called the cops, and of course they said they'd look into it, which of course they wouldn't. Not with all the money the Institute had to throw around.

I dropped Cowboy off at his place around six. Took the professor and Andi to our best (and only) motel around six forty-five. I was dead-dog tired, but hung in the parking lot just long enough to hear the professor rant and rage about the accommodations. After all the drama, I figured I was entitled to a little entertainment. Of course we'd all exchanged phone numbers (my mistake) and agreed to contact each other if someone had an idea, but I wasn't holding my breath.

I got to bed but didn't sleep good. Way too many dreams. First it was the usual suspects—making rent, shop troubles, mom, a guest appearance by Jimmy Jack, who knocked me up at fifteen, and little Monique. Sweet, baby Monique (who I secretly named and held five minutes before the Brady Bunch couple showed up and swept her away). A day doesn't go by that I don't hate myself for that decision, worry about where she is, and how she's being treated. She'll be eleven next month. Same age as the boy I tatted on Cowboy's arm.

The boy that never showed.

But the dream that wrecked me was about Sridhar. He was in one of those cattle chutes they drive sheep through on their way to slaughter. In my version it led to the Institute's auditorium where we all sat watching. Slick was up on stage in his three-piece suit holding sheers. When Sridhar got to him, he shaved off the kid's clothes like wool. And the kid? He just stood there looking at me like I'm supposed to do something.

Once Slick finished and the kid was butt naked, two security guards showed up. They tied his feet and hands and hung him up on a conveyer belt with hooks. It carried him off stage through curtains spattered with blood. I knew what was coming next and forced myself awake . . . both times.

There might have been third, if Cowboy hadn't called.

"Did you get it?" he asked.

"Get what? What time is—"

"The dream. The one me, Andi and the professor got."

"What are you talking about?"

"Where Sridhar is getting butchered?"

Ten minutes later I was in the car driving to pick them up. Besides the dream, a picture kept forming in my head. More like a pattern. I kept pushing it away but it kept coming back. A sign it might be legit. I rummaged through the glove compartment of McD wrappers and parking tickets 'til I found a pen and an envelope from a delinquent water bill.

I sketched as I drove. Pretty simple, really. Just a circle with three spiral arms shooting from it.

I picked Cowboy up first. He gave me that good ol' boy smile. "Mornin' Miss Brenda. How you been?"

Andi greeted me with her usual enthusiasm. "What a fantastic morning. It's great to see you again!"

The professor didn't bother.

We wound up at the local St. Arbucks getting a much needed caffeine fix. Andi chattered the whole time, making me think she'd had a few shots beforehand.

"Since the beginning of time, dreams have been taken seriously by every known people group. The ancient Babylonians put great stock in them. Besides the Persians and the Greeks, there were the Romans. Of course we can't forget the Jews, who even included them in their holy scriptures. Not to mention the Muslims, Christians, and every Eastern belief and culture. In fact, did you know—and you'll find this incredibly interesting— an indigenous tribe of New Guinea once based their entire government upon the dreams of—"

"Your point?" I said as we grabbed our drinks and settled in at a back corner.

"My point is this is definitely not a coincidence. The odds of three people having an identical dream with identical details is nearly impossible."

"Nearly?"

"Approximately one to ten to the one hundred fifty-seventh power."

I gave her a look.

"Approximately," she said.

The professor, who'd been quiet as a tomb, dug a pack of powered creamer from his pocket. He answered my look. "Lactose intolerant."

"So it was Sridhar, right?" Cowboy said. "The little guy put the dream into my brain."

"A wonder he found room," the professor said.

Andi ignored him. "Before his training, Sridhar started off as a lucid dreamer—"

"Which is an entirely different crock of—"

"Which is something the United States government invested millions of dollars developing during the cold war. They called it Remote Viewing and it was somewhat successful."

"The government paid millions of dollars for people to dream?" Cowboy asked.

"I rest my case."

The professor tore open the creamer and dumped it into his coffee. He'd just picked up a stirrer when Andi cried, "Wait! Look!"

We followed her gaze to the professor's cup.

"Did you see that?" she said. "Did you see the way it swirled?"

The professor sighed wearily. "Really?"

"No, I'm serious. No substance swirls into a liquid like that. It was a perfect circle, a perfect ring with three symmetrically placed arms spinning out of it. It lasted only a second, but surely you saw it?"

She turned to Cowboy, who shrugged.

Then to the professor.

He gave the cup an extra stir.

She looked at me. My face must have given something away. "You saw it, didn't you. What did you see, you saw something?"

I pulled out the water bill envelope and shoved it across the table at her.

"There!" She pointed at my sketch. "See! See!"

"See what?" Cowboy asked.

"A nine. Don't you see it? That's the number nine. It doesn't get any clearer than that."

Once she mentioned it, it was kinda clear. A nine, spinning out of the circle.

"And this spiral up here at the top right. See the way it makes a perfect six? And this one at the top left?"

"Another six," Cowboy said.

She tapped the paper. "Nine, six. It was September sixth when we got there last night."

"It still is," Cowboy said. He was catching her enthusiasm. "What about that other six, the one on the left?"

"It could be anything. The minute our plane took off, the number of words in the Institute's name, or—"

"The sixth chair of the sixth graduate in today's ceremony," I said.

Andi and Cowboy looked at me.

"It's a joke," I said. "I wasn't—"

But Andi's eyes were wide. "The sixth day of the ninth month with the sixth participant. It's Sridhar! It's got to be!"

Cowboy frowned. "So, besides the dreams—"

"Someone or something is telling us to help!"

The professor closed his eyes in exaggerated patience.

"That's why we're here!" she practically shouted. "The plane crash, the nine pinnacles, the same numbers over and over again. They're telling us to rescue Sridhar and to rescue him today!"

I shook my head. "You may not have noticed, but we all ready tried that."

Andi reached into her handbag and dug around. "So we have to try again."

"That's right," Cowboy said eagerly. "Practice makes perfect."

She pulled out a pencil and notepad. "We have to devise a plan. Between the four of us there must be some way to save him. Professor? Come on now, we need your help." She drew a rough sketch of the Institute.

The professor looked at me and sighed. Between Cowboy's big-hearted naiveté and Andi's over-the-top enthusiasm, we were outnumbered.

I'll save you the boring details. It was late, but after too many cups of coffee and way too many pastries for breakfast, and then lunch, we had no less than six plans for breaking into the Institute during the ceremony. Because of Cowboy's involvement, most looked like football plays with x's and o's, but at least we had them. One might have actually worked if it weren't for Andi's text message.

"No way," she said, looking at her phone.

"What?" Cowboy asked.

"It's from the Institute." She looked up. "We're on the list."

"List? What list?"

She read it out loud. "'Please stop by Security and pick up your on-campus pass. A fun day to be had by all. Dr. B.J. Trenton.'"

The professor swore under his breath.

It sounded like a pretty good idea and I joined him.

Chapter 9

We're standing at the back wall of the auditorium watching the show. Slick, the real one, had been on stage forty-five minutes rambling on about how privileged the kids were and how they'd be making the world a better place. The good news was they'd shut down the security field so once we got our passes we just strolled on with the rest of the doting parents and whoevers. The bad news was we had to listen to his drivel.

" . . . leaving selfish ambition behind to enter a new fraternity, an order that will guide us from old paradigms of self-destruction and into a new age of knowledge, peace, and prosperity. Graduates, are you ready?"

The six students behind him nodded. Like the others we'd seen the night before, they were strapped into their chairs looking excited and nervous. Except Sridhar. Even where I stood you could tell he was pretty drugged up.

"Then let us begin the induction!"

The choir on the back risers began to sing the same creepy music. Like before, two hooded guys came forward with a long pole. They slipped it into the ring on the pipe's lid and lifted it off. And, like before, glowing green smoke seemed to billow out.

"Arise," Slick called. "Travelers of the future, come fill these newest members who have prepared so long for this moment with your great and wondrous knowledge."

I glance over to the control board a dozen feet away. Some guy in a shaved head was sipping a Jamba Juice and running the show. By the looks of things, everything was going according to plan. Everything but us. We still didn't have one. Even if we did, the two burly guards on either end of the stage could be a problem.

Sridhar and the others watched as the music grew louder and the smoke turned into a cloud that divided into two, then four, with the last two dividing to make six.

"We gotta do something," Cowboy whispered. "Maybe we could ask them to make an announce—"

"Shh," Andi said. "Listen."

He paused a second. "All I hear is singing."

"Exactly."

"What's that got to do with—"

"Shh. Don't you hear that? The rhythm? The pattern?"

"It's just music."

"And a rather loose description of the term," the professor added.

"No, listen." She took a breath and blew it out. "Hear it?"

We didn't.

She did it again—breathed in and out. She motioned to the stage and did it a third time. "See? See how Sridhar and the other five are aligning their breathing with the music?"

"To help them relax." I said. "Like the guy told us last night."

"But those bass notes, hear their rhythm? The way they throb? Underneath?" She tapped her fingers into her palm. "Bum-bum, bum-bum, bum-bum . . ."

"It's like a heartbeat," Cowboy said.

"Precisely. And it's lined up to match the light pulsing inside those clouds."

I looked on as Sridhar and the other kids closed their eyes and tipped their heads back. "So it *is* to help them relax," I said.

The professor shook his head. "No. It's to manipulate their limbic systems."

"English?" I said.

"It's creating a trance-like state. Lowering their resistance, making them susceptible to hypnotic suggestion."

"Or to whatever wants to enter them," Andi added.

I turned back to the stage. The clouds were moving into position over each of the students. "So what do we do?"

"If we're to help Sridhar, we better act now," Andi said, "or it'll be too late."

I gestured to Shaved Head at the control panel. "We could take over the board." I turned to Cowboy. "You could take him out, right?"

He shook his head. "I wouldn't want to hurt him."

"You take out guys every week on the football field."

"Not on purpose. If I do, I always try to patch 'em up when I'm done."

I just looked at him.

"There's another way," Andi said. "If I go backstage and confuse the singers' rhythm, if I can shift it so it's actually conflicting with the flashing clouds—"

The professor scoffed. "You think you can create enough dissonance to break their hypnotic state?"

"And disrupt the ceremony? Maybe."

He dropped his head and shook it in disbelief.

"And then what?" I said.

"I don't know. If there's enough confusion, maybe Tank could sneak in from backstage. Maybe he could free Sridhar and get him out of there."

"And maybe pigs can fly," the professor said.

I looked down at the stage. The clouds were over the students' heads and pulsing brighter. The kids were beginning to open their mouths.

"We have to do something," Andi said. "Does anyone have a better idea?"

We didn't.

"All right, then. Tank, you come with me." He nodded and they headed for the backdoor to the hallway circling the arena.

I looked at the professor. He leaned against the

wall, as non-committal as ever. I turned back to the control board and Shaved Head. Andi's plan was iffy at best. It wouldn't hurt to have a back up.

I headed for the board.

There was a four-foot wall around it. The closer I got, the more Shaved Head looked big and impressive. But I had a few impressive attributes of my own.

Once I got there I tugged down on my V-neck, making sure they were visible.

"Psst!" I whispered. "Hey!"

He glanced up from the board.

I smiled and leaned forward, making sure I had his full attention. He crossed to me.

"Can I watch?" I whispered.

He frowned.

I motioned him closer and whispered into his ear. "I really think it's hot the way you run all this stuff." He looked at me. I nodded and mouthed "*Really hot.*" He broke into a smile that had most of its teeth.

I reached for the little gate separating us. "Can I watch?"

He hesitated.

I smiled, tugged at my shirt again. He opened the gate.

Happy to show off his manly prowess, he returned to work. Happy to find an external hard drive, I slammed it into the back of his head. He slid to the floor. No one noticed—except the professor, who almost looked impressed.

I turned to the board with all its switches and blinking lights. Where to begin?

Up on stage, Andi had slipped beside the last choir member and was singing her little heart out. You couldn't hear her, but you could see the choir staring. Slick, too. No one was happy.

The professor arrived and pushed open the gate to join me.

I nodded to the stage. "How's she doing?"

He listened and shook his head. "Not enough."

I motioned to the board. "Plan B?"

He nodded. "Shut her down."

"Any idea how?"

He didn't have a clue. Well, except for Shaved Head's Jamba Juice. The one he picked up (Tropical Fruit, I believe), and poured over the board.

It was like the Fourth of July—lights and sparks everywhere. And not just the board. The whole auditorium went dark. When the emergency lights came on, one of the security guards spotted us and took off up the steps.

"Now what?" the professor said.

My solution wasn't as original as his but probably just as effective.

"Run!"

Chapter 10

I went for one back door. The professor took the other. By the time I circled around and got to the stage, things had definitely changed. For starters, the clouds were shorting out. The images kept repeating themselves, floating from the pipe to the students, from the pipe to the students. The choir had quit singing and the audience was anything but happy.

"A hoax?" Someone yelled. "This is all a hoax?"

Another shouted, "We've been watching a light show?"

Of course Slick did his best to fix things. "Please, we're currently having some technical difficulties."

And all the teachers, about a dozen in the front row, were on their feet trying to quiet everyone.

Cowboy had unstrapped Sridhar and was holding off the other guard. "Please. I don't want to hurt you," he kept saying. "We'll just be takin' this boy and be on our way."

I moved to the kid and helped him to his feet.

"What happened?" he mumbled. "What's going on?"

Slick spotted us. "Stop them!"

"You two best be going, Miss Brenda," Cowboy said.

I looked into the auditorium and saw the other guard coming for us.

"What about—"

"I'll be there in a jiffy. Me and the fellas just need a little talk."

I looked over to see Andi waving from the side exit. "Over here!"

The kid and I started toward her. The lights flickered again. The crowd had grown even more restless and was getting to their feet.

"My child wasted two years of her life here?"

"A fraud. This is all a fraud!"

"You'll be hearing from my lawyers."

"I *am* a lawyer!"

Slick and the teachers definitely had their hands full. Still, he managed to shout at us. "I've engaged the security field, so you're going nowhere!"

We joined Andi and stepped into the hallway as Slick repeated, "I said you're going no—"

The door slammed shut behind us.

We crossed the hallway and opened the exit door. The yard was in front of us. The gate forty feet away.

"Now what?" I said.

"We followed a spiral," Andi said.

"What?"

"Last night, we circled the building. We followed a spiral path to this location."

"A path we can't see without those special glasses." I turned to the kid. "Unless you got them now."

He shook his head.

"Wait a minute!" Andi said. "That pattern you drew of the numbers? The one identical to the creamer in the professor's coffee? Do you have it?"

I pulled the envelope from my pocket and handed it to her.

"Yes!" she cried.

"What?"

"The route."

"That's no route. It's numbers and dates. You said so yourself."

"And it's the route."

"It can't be both."

"Maybe not in three dimensions. But if Trenton is correct about multiple dimensions, then of course it is."

"Of course?"

"Multiple dimensions function at multiple levels. Therefore they should have multiple meanings. They *must* have multiple meanings." She pointed where the arc of the number met the circle. "If this is our current location, we must follow this exact route back to the gate."

It made no sense to me. So what else was new?

The door opened. Lots of noise came from inside as Cowboy stepped out.

"The guards?" I asked. "They cool?"

"They'll be a little cranky when they wake up, but yes ma'am, everything's good."

"And the professor?" Andi said.

"Right behind me."

"Let's go, then." Andi held out the diagram as we headed into the yard. We'd gone about twenty feet when the professor showed up at the door.

"Wait for me!" he yelled.

"The path," Andi shouted. "Avoid the field by following our path."

The old guy froze. Guess he didn't want an encore of last night's performance.

I saw where we'd been. "Keep going," I said. "I'll go back and get him."

"Stay on the path," Andi repeated.

I nodded. When I arrived, the professor was his usual sunny self. "I hope she knows where she's going."

The lights in the building beside us flickered.

"What did you do?" I said.

"There was some extra Jamba Juice."

"And?"

"I found the main circuit room."

We headed after the others. We got about half way when the door flew open and both security guards piled out.

"Let's move." I grabbed the professor's arm and pulled him along faster.

"Be careful," he groused. "Stay on the path! Careful!"

The guards gained on us. The fact they didn't drag around a whiney windbag made it easier. That, and their John Lennon glasses.

Andi, Cowboy, and the kid reached the gate. We were just feet behind them when I suddenly thought of baby Monique. Only now she wasn't a baby. She was the same age she'd be today. They had her locked in some dark room. A closet. And she was sobbing. Her face streaked with tears. All alone.

It was only a thought, but so real I had to gasp, "Monique . . ."

Over her tears I heard another voice. Old and white: "You'll stay in there until you wash *all* those dishes."

"Momma?" she cried. But not for them. For me. "Momma!"

I could barely catch my breath. "Monique, is that—"

"No!" The professor yelled. I looked up to see him grab his head. "Not again! Somebody help me!"

"They changed the security field!" Andi shouted.

"Momma . . ." More images flickered. Sharper. Clearer. Monique stood barefoot in a cold, wet cellar. She was shivering. Hard. Her arms raised. To me! "Momma? Momma, help me!"

"Oh, baby—"

"Grab my hand, Professor!" Andi shouted. "Grab my—"

"I can't remember!" he cried. "I don't—"

"Grab my hand!"

"Miss Brenda!" Cowboy yelled.

I blinked. Saw Cowboy reaching for me. He was six feet away. The professor was beside me, doubled over.

"Miss Brenda!"

I fought off Monique's image long enough to grab the professor by the waist.

"Help me!" he cried. "Help—"

It took all my strength, but I flung him past me. He stumbled out of the field and into Andi's arms.

"Momma!"

I spun back to Monique.

"Momma, it hurts. Momma, they're hurting me! Momma—"

"Miss Brenda!"

I tried focusing on Cowboy's voice, pushing her out of my mind. But I couldn't. How could I, when what I feared most was happening right in front of me?

Chapter 11

"Father, please . . . please, forgive me!" Monique huddled in the corner of a fancy bedroom. Stuffed animals. Canopy bed. Everything pink and frilly. "I'm sorry, please . . ."

A human tub of lard stood over her, belt in hand.

"It was an accident, I—"

Slap. He hit her hard across the face. I felt the sting on my own. I grabbed my cheek and staggered forward. "Monique!"

"I'll teach you to respect my property."

Slap!

"Miss Brenda!" Cowboy's voice was far away.

"Think of somethin' good!"

Now Monique was looking out a window. Rain streaked it. Her face was wet with tears. Outside, the Brady Bunch loaded their brats into a van, preparing to drive away.

"Momma . . ." She choked out the word. "Momma, where are you?"

I stood at the door, tears in my own eyes. "Right here, baby. I'm right here."

"Fight it, girl!" The professor's voice called . "It's an illusion, fight it!"

He was right. I concentrated with all I had to push her out of my head.

The image flickered.

I tried harder.

She disappeared.

I turned around and saw Andi, eight feet away, reaching for me. "Hurry!"

I started forward, two, three steps before I heard, "Momma . . ."

She sounded so real. So lost. I knew I shouldn't, but I had to.

"Miss Brenda!"

I turned and there she was. So alone. So frightened.

"Oh, baby." I started forward. "Momma's right here."

"Brenda!"

I was nearly there. Stretching out my arms. Suddenly her face darkened, twisted into rage. "Stay back!"

"Baby—"

"I hate you!"

I slowed. "Sweetheart, I—"

"I hate you! I'll always hate you!"

I stopped.

She kept shouting. "You gave me away! To strangers, you gave me away!"

"No, I—"

"Like garbage! You threw me away!"

"Miss Brenda?"

I closed my eyes. Trying to force her out of my mind.

"And now I have to suffer. My whole life I'm suffering."

But the harder I tried, the stronger she became.

"It's your fault. It's all your fault!"

I heard Sridhar's voice, faint. "You cannot remove it. You must replace it!"

"Think of somethin' good, Miss Brenda. Replace it with somethin' good."

"You've ruined me. You've ruined everything!"

"Somethin' good."

"I hate you!" The words punched me in the gut. "I hate everything about you!"

"Think of somethin' good!"

I thought of her delivery, back in the hospital. Not the pain, but afterwards.

"A girl, Ms. Barnick. " The doctor smiled down at me. "A beautiful, baby girl."

I remembered her tiny weight when they put her on my belly. Her warmth. The crying, the squirming. She was a part of me, but more. Another human. Completely me, completely different.

"You gave me away . . ." Her voice began to fade.

I thought of her eyes. Those puffy slits squinting against the light. People say newborns can't focus, but she saw me. She opened them and looked right at me.

And we connected. Mother and child. My heart swelled.

"Miss Brenda!"

I turned to see Cowboy and the others motioning to me.

"Hurry!"

I took a step toward them, still seeing my baby, still hearing her cry. Another step. The crying stopped for an instant and she smiled. At me. Another step. I was smiling too, my heart bursting . . . as I took the final step and fell into Cowboy's arms.

"You okay?" he asked.

The memory faded. I nodded and he helped me to my feet.

Suddenly Sridhar screamed. I turned around to see the kid grabbing the back of his neck and doubling over.

"Did you honestly think you could leave that easily?"

I turned and saw Slick standing in the middle of the field, glasses on, definitely not happy. He pressed a small remote in his hand. The kid dropped to his knees, shrieking in pain.

"And without even saying goodbye?"

"Stop it!" Andi yelled. "You're killing him. You're killing him!"

"He should be so lucky."

Chapter 12

"Please—" The kid gasped.

Slick showed no mercy. "You're the first, did you know that? The only graduate to ever refuse induction."

Lights from another building flickered, then went out.

"You think we wouldn't make an example of you?"

"I'll . . . come back. I'll—"

"It's a little late for that." He cranked up whatever gizmo he had in his hand. The kid cried out, curling into a ball, trying to breathe.

"Stop it! Andi yelled.

"He's just a boy." Cowboy shouted.

Slick ignored them. "You have no idea who you're dealing with, do you?"

"Release him," the professor called. "Release the boy and we will go."

Slick broke out laughing. "Go? Oh, you'll go, all right. But trust me, you won't be leaving. Not this war."

"War?" Andi shouted. "What war?"

"Do you think you four were brought together by accident? Are you really so naïve as to think there are not greater forces at work here?"

"What are—"

"Please . . . " the kid whimpered, gasping.

"You'll not succeed. They're too powerful. You may have won the battle but the war has barely be—"

He was cut off by a muffled explosion at one end of the auditorium and a small puff of smoke rising. At the same time, the kid groaned and seemed to relax. Apparently the pain had stopped.

Slick wasn't so lucky. "Ahh!" He doubled over. "No!"

We traded looks.

"The security field?" Andi asked.

The professor frowned. "It must be shorting out."

"No! No . . ."

Cowboy shook his head. "I don't think—"

"I've done everything you've asked!" Slick cried. "I've—" He began to stagger. "No!" He threw up his arms, slapping away at something no one could see. "No!"

"Those are some ugly fears," I said.

He fell to his knees and began choking, gagging.

"Them ain't fears, Miss Brenda."

"Stop this!" A different voice sounded. It came from Slick, but it was deep, guttural. "Stop this at once!"

Slick's normal voice came back, pleading. "No . . . don't—"

"Stop!" The other voice started cussing. Worse than me on a bad day.

Slick's hands shot to his face. He began scratching at it, clawing, until it was covered in blood. He spun back to us, his eyes wild. "Help me! Help—"

"Shut up!" the deeper voice yelled. "You are a failure!"

"No! No, I did every—" He screamed and threw himself on the ground where he began to writhe.

"That's enough!" Cowboy shouted. We turned to him. Before any of us could stop him, he stepped back into the field.

"Tank!" Andi called.

"Ain't nobody deserve that," he said, and kept walking forward.

"Cowboy!"

He kept right on going. You could tell he was hurting. His back was to us, but you could tell something real bad was running through his head. He stumbled, almost lost his balance.

"Tank!"

But he kept pushing forward. The air over the yard crackled like electricity. For the briefest second it filled with sparks.

Cowboy staggered, but kept right on walking.

It happened again, crackling louder and longer. Sparks, like glitter, filled the air.

I turned to Andi, but she didn't have a clue.

"He's overloading it," the professor yelled.

"He's what?"

"Whatever he's thinking, he's overloading the system."

"That's not possible."

"Tell *him* that."

I turned back to Cowboy. He kept walking. The crackling got louder. The sparks brighter. Finally he reached Slick.

By now the man was screaming uncontrollably, convulsing and rolling on the ground. Cowboy knelt down to him. He took him by the shoulders and said something so soft no one but Slick heard. The man showed his appreciation by spitting in the big boy's face. Cowboy barely noticed. He just kept on holding Slick and talking.

And Slick kept on struggling. But it did no good. He gradually got weaker and weaker until he finally wore himself out. When he quit struggling, Cowboy let him go. But the man wasn't done. He threw up his fists and began beating on Cowboy's chest and shoulders, tried punching his face, all the time screaming and swearing. Cowboy was unfazed. He just grabbed Slick again, held him, and kept talking.

Slick's eyes bulged in frustration but he couldn't move. His face grew red. The veins in his neck bulged. It looked like he was going to explode. Then he threw back his head and let go a chilling scream. A howl like an animal's. It went on until he ran out of air.

He finally collapsed into Cowboy's arms. This time it was real.

The air over the yard stopped crackling and sparking.

"Tank?" Andi shouted. "Tank, are you all right?"

The big guy turned to us.

We all waited.

He broke into that good ol' boy grin of his. Then he scooped Slick up into his arms and rose to his feet.

Epilogue

The 130-mile drive to Bakersfield was as long as it was boring. I didn't mind. Not this time. It was the first peace I'd had since our visit to the Twilight Zone. A couple weeks had passed since our fun and games at the Institute.

Of course Cowboy had carried Slick to their infirmary. And of course they threw us out, with promises we'd be hearing from their attorneys. Not that I blamed them. Between the professor's electrical work and Cowboy's voodoo, we'd pretty much destroyed the place. At least their credibility.

I wish I could give you a "happily ever after," but it didn't roll that way. The evening we finished, Andi and Professor Sunshine took a taxi to the airport. He had lectures at UCLA the following day—which left no time for long goodbyes, which I'd try to get over.

Cowboy wasn't so easy to get rid of. But I'll get to him in a minute.

It was the kid, Sridhar, that haunted me. I let him stay on my sofa the first couple of nights—back when he was calling his folks in Sri Lanka for money to fly home. But they never connected. They'd either moved or changed their number. The kid didn't buy it for a minute. Something else was up. To keep him safe, we made plans to ship him to my mom's over in Arizona. It never happened.

He disappeared. Just like that. One morning his blankets were folded, the pillows stacked, and he was gone. My first thought was the Institute. I called the police. They said I had to file a missing persons report.

"Can you at least drive out there and check?" I said.

"You think he's at the Institute?" a board voice asked.

"That's what I said."

"So if you know where he is, how can he be missing?"

I hung up and drove out there myself.

I wasn't sure what I'd do. It didn't matter. When I got there the place was deserted. Completely. In seventy-two hours everyone had pulled up and disappeared. The gate was open, the auditorium gutted, the classrooms and dormitories empty. A ghost town. Talk about eerie. That night, first time in a long time, I locked my doors.

A few mornings later Cowboy swung by the shop.

He wanted me to touch up his tat where it had scabbed.

As he sat in the chair he said, "He didn't leave a note or nothin'?"

I shook my head and began inking.

He kept sitting there thinking, or whatever he does when he isn't talking. Finally he said, "You ever wonder what that headmaster guy meant when he said we weren't brought together by accident?"

I did, but kept my mouth shut.

Cowboy didn't. Or couldn't. He looked down at my work. "I miss 'em already, don't you?"

"Not exactly."

He motioned to the boy that I'd tatted with the four of us. "You ever wonder about this little guy?"

"I just ink what I see." I finished up and began smearing on the Aquaphor. "I got a question for you."

"Shoot."

"How come that security field never bothered you?"

"What do you mean?"

"I mean it put me and the professor through hell. It barely touched you."

"Oh, yeah it did. Something fierce."

"'Til you replaced what you were afraid of with something better."

"That's right."

"Which was?"

He didn't answer.

I taped on the cellophane. "What'd you replace your fear with, Cowboy?

He broke into that goofy grin. "If I told you, you'd just say I'm preaching."

"What'd you replace it with?"

"God. I kept thinking how much He loves— Ow! That's tender."

I didn't bother to apologize. "Somebody still owes me one fifty for this."

"I'll take care of it."

"Plus another twenty for interest."

"Yes, ma'am."

"Alright, we're done here." I peeled off my gloves.

He climbed out of the chair. That's when he spotted the envelope with the numbers or the symbol or whatever it was that I'd sketched and left on the counter.

"Wow," he said, moving closer.

"Wow, what?"

"Did you ever notice that if you turn this around it's not a six, a nine, and a six? If you keep turning, it's a six, a six and another six."

"And thanks for stopping by." I ushered him towards the door.

"I'll drop off the check tomorrow."

"Mail's fine."

That had been two weeks ago.

I parked the car six blocks from the Bakersfield airport. It was gonna make me a little late, but it was worth it, not paying for parking. I cleared security and headed for my gate. Some organization I'd never heard of up in Washington State had e-mailed me. They said they'd seen my work and wanted to discuss building a franchise. It was obviously a mistake, but not mine. So when they wired me a couple hundred and e-mailed me the ticket, I figured let them worry about it. A little vacation wouldn't hurt.

At least that's what I thought 'til I heard the voices

at the gate.

"This treatment is unacceptable. You should have been aware of the weather long before we departed, long before you dumped us in this godforsaken . . . where are we again?"

"Bakersfield, Professor."

"Bakersfield."

The professor was fighting with the attendant behind the counter, Andi beside him.

"Sir, please try to understand. First class is entirely booked. There is no possible way to—"

"Look at this ticket!" the professor said. "Do you see it? What does it say?"

"First class, but—"

"We had first class out of Los Angeles and we expect first class out of, out of . . ."

"Bakersfield, Professor."

I got in the boarding line and turned my head so they wouldn't see me. Too late.

"Oh, look, there's Brenda!"

I pretended not to hear. But Andi was as persistent as she was cheery. "Brenda. Brenda!"

When it was clear everybody heard her but me, I turned and acted surprised. "Hey."

"Are you on this flight, too?"

I nodded. "What are the odds?"

"A good question. I'll let you know."

"I bet you will."

"Pardon me?"

I shook my head.

"We'll see you on board, okay?"

"Right."

Once I got on the plane I moved down the aisle, checking my seat number. The good news was I was way in the back. With luck, the professor would get his way and wind up in first class. The bad news was—

"Miss Brenda! Miss Brenda!"

I looked up. There was Cowboy in the last row, all grins.

"What are you doing here?" I said.

"It's incredible. The University of Washington, they want me to fly up there and talk to them."

"Talk to them?" I continued down the aisle toward him.

"For a scholarship! They want to talk to me about a scholarship."

I glanced at my ticket, fear growing.

"Think of it. I might become an honest to goodness Husky! Go dawgs! Isn't that fantastic? Isn't God good?"

"Well, he's something."

"What seat do you have?"

"Thirty-eight D."

"Are you kidding me? I have 38 E!"

I searched for another empty seat. Any would do. But I was late and the plane was packed.

"Did you see the professor and Andi? They're on the same flight, too. Isn't that amazing?"

I stuffed my backpack into the overhead. With no place to go, I dropped into the seat beside him.

"This is so cool. I mean, really, really cool."

I sighed and buckled in. Like so many times before, Slick's voice echoed in my head. *Are you so naïve as to think there are not greater forces at work?*

Cowboy continued his chatter. "I mean really, when you stop to think about it, how lucky can we get?"

I leaned back and closed my eyes, knowing what ever was happening, whatever was going on . . . it had nothing to do with luck.

Soli Deo gloria.

FROM HARBINGERS 2
THE HAUNTED

FRANK PERETTI

Clyde Morris looked entirely the part of a wraith: neck tendons tuned like a harp, white hair wild, fogging corneas following unseen demons about the old dining room. "My life, my years, all over. Done! Can't reach them from here, can't change them, no more chances!"

His frumpish wife Nadine could make no sense of his ravings, his clenching and unclenching hands, his rising, pacing, sitting again, his seeing horrible things. She reached across the table to touch him, but drew her hand back—it felt chilled as with frost.

He leaned, nearly lunged over the table, his face close to hers. "It knows me! It knows all about me!"

From down the hall came the shriek of door hinges. Clyde's eyes rolled toward the sound, his veiny face contorted. A wind rustled the curtains, fluttered a newspaper, swung the chandelier so it jingled.

Clyde stood and the wind hit him broadside, pushing him toward the hall.

"Clyde!"

He reached across the space between them but the wind, roaring, carried him down the hall along with cushions, newspapers, the tablecloth.

A doorway in the hall, glowing furnace red, pulled him. He craned forward to fight it, stumbled, grappled, and slid backward toward it.

The doorway sucked him in like a dust particle. A high-pitched scream faded into infinite distance until cut off when the door slammed shut.

The wind stopped. The newspaper pages settled to the floor. A doily fluttered down like a snowflake. The chandelier jingled through two diminishing swings, then stopped jingling and hung still.

Now the only sound was the wailing of the widow, flung to the floor in the old Victorian house.

OTHER BOOKS BY BILL MYERS

NOVELS
Child's Play
The Judas Gospel
The God Hater
The Voice
Angel of Wrath
The Wager
Soul Tracker
The Presence
The Seeing
The Face of God
When the Last Leaf Falls
Eli
Blood of Heaven
Threshold
Fire of Heaven

NON-FICTION
The Jesus Experience—Journey Deeper into the Heart of God
Supernatural Love
Supernatural War

CHILDREN BOOKS
Baseball for Breakfast (picture book)
The Bug Parables (picture book series)
Bloodstone Chronicles (fantasy series)
McGee and Me (book/video series)
The Incredible Worlds of Wally McDoogle (comedy series)
Bloodhounds, Inc. (mystery series)
The Elijah Project (supernatural suspense series)

Secret Agent Dingledorf and His Trusty Dog Splat (comedy series)
TJ and the Time Stumblers (comedy series)
Truth Seekers (action adventure series)

TEEN BOOKS
Forbidden Doors (supernatural suspense)
Dark Power Collection
Invisible Terror Collection
Deadly Loyalty Collection
Ancient Forces Collection

For a complete list of Bill's books, sample chapters, and newsletter signup go to www.Billmyers.com Or check out his Facebook page: www.facebook.com/billmyersauthor .

Don't miss the next books in the Harbingers series:

***The Haunted*, by Frank Peretti.**

The Sentinels, by Angela Hunt

The Girl, by Alton Gansky

CPSIA information can be obtained at www.ICGtesting.com
Printed in the USA
LVOW10s2159240816

501735LV00014B/291/P